MW01026984

The Kim, Kari, & Kevin Storybook

Kay Kuzma

Illustrated by Elfred Lee

REVIEW AND HERALD® PUBLISHING ASSOCIATION
HAGERSTOWN, MD 21740

Copyright © 1979 and 1997 by
Kay Kuzma
International copyright secured

The author assumes full responsibility for the accuracy of all
facts and quotations as cited in this book.

This book was
Edited by Jeannette R. Johnson
Designed by Patricia S. Wegh
Cover designed by Willie S. Duke
Illustrations by Elfred Lee
Typeset: Clearface Regular 13/16

PRINTED IN U.S.A.

01 00 99 98 97   5 4 3 2 1

R&H Cataloging Service
Kuzma, Kay Judeen (Humpal), 1941-
      The Kim, Kari, and Kevin storybook.

      1. Values.   2. Child rearing.   3. Child development.
4. Children—Conduct of life.   I. Title..

                  303.32

ISBN 0-8280-1104-4

Dedication

I dedicate this book to my children,
Kim, Kari, and Kevin, who lived these pages
before there was a script,
and to Jennifer Ruskjer,
Andrea Bryson, and Jonathan Lee,
who reenacted these stories.
May the recording of these childhood scenes
have a small part in helping them
and children everywhere
develop beautiful characters.

Contents

Introduction

Developing wholesome character traits in young children is a task that confronts parents and teachers alike. The experiences of childhood help shape each person into the kind of individual he or she will be as an adult. One important avenue is children's literature. The stories children read, or hear read to them, are often influential years later as they make decisions that will affect their character.

This book has been designed to accompany the volume *Building Character,* by Jan and Kay Kuzma. The same 13 character traits that are discussed in that book are illustrated by the stories in this volume.

The very first chapter is about faithfulness (faith), because children must first develop faith and confidence in their parents before they can develop other positive character traits. Next is orderliness. Without orderliness or consistency a child has difficulty developing faith. Once these two character traits are established, the others follow: self-discipline, happiness, perseverance, honesty, thoughtfulness, efficiency, responsibility, self-respect, enthusiasm, humility, and peacefulness. These are the traits my husband and I chose to emphasize with our children. In the final chapter, I end where I began—in faithfulness—this time emphasizing trust in God.

The stories are based upon incidents in the lives of our children, Kim, Kari, and Kevin. We have had a delightful time telling these stories around the family circle. Now as we share these stories with you, we hope that your children will enjoy them and benefit from them as much as our children have.

Meet Kim, Kari, and Kevin

In a little green house,
   in the middle of an orange grove,
      there lived a daddy,
         and a mommy,
            and three special children.

Kim was the biggest. Kim was 5 years old. "I'm almost 6," she would say, if anyone asked.

Kevin was the littlest. Kevin was 2. If anyone

asked him how old he was, he would hold up two fingers.

Kari wasn't the biggest, and Kari wasn't the littlest. Kari was in between. Kari was like the ice cream in an ice-cream sandwich. Kari was 4 years old.

In a little green house,
in the middle of an orange grove,
there lived a daddy,
and a mommy,
and three special children,
and they loved each other very much.

9

Dear Grandma,
We Need Gum

When Grandma sent a letter addressed to Kim, Kari, and Kevin, it was always a very special letter.

It wasn't a thin envelope with just paper in it. It was a fat envelope with gum in it.

One piece was for Kim.

One piece was for Kari.

And one piece was for Kevin.

Sometimes the gum was fruit-flavored gum.

Sometimes it was cinnamon-flavored gum.

Sometimes it was pink bubble gum.

But whatever kind it was, it was always sugarless.

And it always tasted "scrumptious."

"Mommy, may we have some gum?" asked Kim, Kari, and Kevin one day.

"If I had some gum, I would give it to you. But there isn't any."

"But we want some."

"I'm sorry," said Mommy.

"Maybe Grandma will send us a letter today," said Kim. "Then we would have some gum."

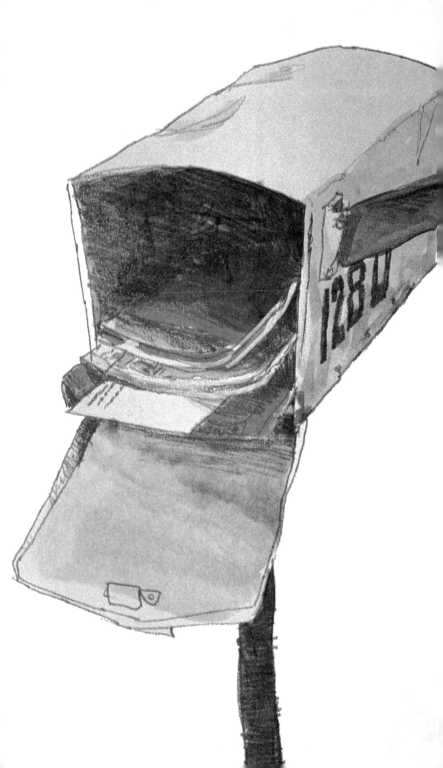

The children went out to the mailbox. They opened it. The mailbox was full.

There were two magazines,

five thin letters,

and one fat envelope.

But the fat envelope had Daddy's name on it. There wasn't any letter from Grandma.

The next day the children felt sure there would be a letter waiting for them. They went out to the mailbox. They opened it. The mailbox was full.

There was one newspaper advertisement,

three thin letters,

and one fat envelope.

But the fat envelope had Mommy's name on it. There wasn't any letter from Grandma.

"Maybe we had better write to Grandma," Kim said, "and tell her we need some gum."

"That's a good idea," said Kari.

Kim got the paper and pencil.

Kari got the envelope.

Kevin got the stamp.

Kim wrote in big, neat letters:

DEAR GRANDMA,

WE NEED GUM.

LOVE, KIM, KARI, KEVIN

Kari folded the letter and put it into the envelope and licked it shut.

Kevin licked the stamp and put it in the corner of the envelope—upside down.

They asked Mommy to write Grandma's address

on the envelope. And then they put the envelope in the mailbox.

"Now," said Kari, "maybe tomorrow Grandma will send us some gum."

"It takes a long time for a letter to get to Colorado," said Kim, "and if Grandma doesn't have any gum in the house, she will have to go to the store and buy some. Then she will have to put it in an envelope and send it to us. And it takes a long time for a letter to get to California."

"What if she doesn't send any gum?" asked Mommy.

"Grandma will send us the gum," said Kim, Kari, and Kevin, "especially when she knows we need it."

Every day the children checked the mailbox. "No letter from Grandma today," they would say.

Then early one morning Kim said, "I think we will get the letter from Grandma today."

"What makes you think so?" asked Mommy.

"Because, if it takes two days for our letter to get to Colorado and one day for Grandma to buy the gum and two days for Grandma's letter to get to California, that makes five days. And today is the day."

The children went out to the mailbox. They opened it. The mailbox was full.

There was one magazine,
    one newspaper advertisement,
        four thin letters,
           and one fat envelope.

And the envelope was addressed to KIM, KARI, AND KEVIN KUZMA.

"It's here!" they yelled. "Grandma sent us our gum!"

And when they opened the envelope,
out fell six pieces of gum.

An orange and a cherry stick for Kim.

A cinnamon and grape stick for Kari.

And two pieces of pink bubble gum for Kevin.

"How did you know there was going to be gum in the envelope?" asked Mommy.

16

"Because it was from Grandma, and Grandma always sends us gum—especially when we need it."

Then Kim, Kari, and Kevin got another piece of
     paper, and a pencil,
          and an envelope,
               and a stamp,
and sent another letter to Grandma.

This time Kim wrote in big, neat letters:
          DEAR GRANDMA,
          THANK YOU FOR THE GUM.
          LOVE, KIM, KARI, KEVIN

18

One, Two, Where Is My Shoe?

"Shoes, shoes,
  Here and there.
  Why can't I
  Find a pair?"

muttered Kari as she sorted through a large pile of
shoes in the shoe drawer in her bedroom.

"Hurry, Kari," called Mommy. "The stores will be
closing soon, and we have a lot of shopping to do."

"I'm coming, Mommy, just as soon as I find
some shoes.

"One is red.
  One is blue.
  One is brown.
  Aren't there two?"

muttered Kari as she dug deeper into the drawer.

"Hurry, Kari," called Mommy. "The stores will be
closing soon, and we have a lot of shopping to do."

"I'm coming, Mommy, just as soon as I find some shoes.

"One is white.
Another one too.
Put them on.
This won't do!"

muttered Kari as she tried to put two left shoes on her right and left feet.

"Hurry, Kari," called Mommy. "The stores will be closing soon, and we have a lot of shopping to do."

"Sandals and sneakers.
Stripes and plaids.
One is Kevin's.
One is Dad's!"

muttered Kari as she found a shoe of Daddy's! She had been wearing it to play mailman and had forgotten to put it in his closet.

"Hurry, Kari," called Mommy. "The stores will be closing soon, and we have a lot of shopping to do."

"I'm coming, Mommy, just as soon as I find some shoes.

"There's a black one.
Another one too.
I'll put them on.
That's what I'll do!"

muttered Kari as she quickly put on the shoes, and called, "I'm coming, Mommy."

But flip-flop, slip-slop, plip-plop went the shoes as she tried to walk. They were too big. They belonged to Kim. What should she do?

"Hurry, Kari," called Mommy. "The stores will be closing soon, and we have a lot of shopping to do." Mommy was already waiting in the car, and there was nothing else for Kari to do but to get into the car with her flip-flopping, slip-slopping, plip-plopping shoes.

Mommy went shopping and Kari went flip-flopping after her. Finally they stopped at a shoe store. Mommy didn't need any shoes. Kari didn't need any shoes. She had plenty at home. She just couldn't find them. But Mommy went in, and Kari flip-flopped behind her.

They sat down and a clerk said, "May I help you?"

"No, thank you," said Mommy. "We're just looking."

"What are we looking at?" asked Kari.

"Shoes—just shoes," said Mommy. "Rows and rows of shoes—
red ones,
blue ones,
　　green ones,
　　　　yellow ones,
　　　　　pink ones,
　　　　　　white ones,
　　　　　　　brown ones,
　　　　　　　　black ones,
　　　　　　　　　plaid ones,
　　　　　　　　　　striped ones,
　　　　　　　　　　　and even purple
　　　　　　　　　　　ones—

with the left and the right shoe, side by side."

When Kari got home, she went straight to her bedroom and kicked off the flip-flopping, slip-slop-ping, plip-plopping shoes and picked them up and put the left and right shoe side by side in Kim's closet.

Then she looked under the bed. There was a right blue shoe. She picked it up and found a left blue shoe in the pile of shoes in the shoe drawer and placed them side by side in her closet.

Then she looked under the sofa,
    behind the chair,
       on top of the desk,
         and on the shelf, until she had found all her shoes and placed the left by the right, side by side, in her closet.

When she finished the job, she ran to Mommy. "Mommy, may I wear a pair of your shoes?"

"Oh, Kari, can't you find your shoes yet?" Mommy sighed.

"I found all my shoes," said Kari, "but now I want to pretend I'm the mommy and take my little girl to the shoe store."

So Kari chose a nice red pair of Mommy's shoes and pretended to take her little girl shopping. While she waited for the pretend clerk to help them, she sang

> "One, two.
>
> Left, right.
>
> Put them back.
>
> Just right!"

And when she was finished playing, she put Mommy's red shoes back in Mommy's closet, side by side—just right. And never again did Kari have to mutter

> "One, two.
>
> Where's my shoe?"

Wide-awake Kim

Everyone knows 8:00 is bedtime for children, at least for little children. Everyone, that is, except Kim. Kim was always wide-awake when Mommy said, "It's 8:00—bedtime."

Little brother Kevin wasn't wide-awake. He went to bed at 7:15 every night. But that wasn't the only time he slept. He took a nap every afternoon.

Kim's younger sister, Kari, wasn't wide-awake. She always went to bed at 7:30. Mommy didn't even have to tell her it was bedtime. She just couldn't keep her eyes open any longer. Sometimes Kari even fell asleep in funny places, like at the supper table, when she didn't take her afternoon nap.

But Kim knew Mommy and Daddy didn't go to bed at 8:00. Eight o'clock was just the time Mommy was finishing washing the supper dishes and was sitting down in her favorite chair to read.

Eight o'clock was just the time that Daddy finished feeding the dog and was sitting down in his favorite chair to listen to his special records.

"Kim, it's 8:00—bedtime," Mommy would call.

"But, Mommy, I'm not sleepy. I'm wide-awake. Please read me another story."

So Mommy would read Kim another story.

And then Daddy would call from the other room, "Kim, it's 8:15—time for little girls to go to bed."

"But, Daddy, I'm not sleepy. I'm wide-awake.

Rock me a little bit." So Daddy would rock Kim in the big, cozy rocker.

And then Mommy would call, "Kim, it's 8:30—bedtime." And Daddy would say, "That's right, bedtime, Kim."

"But I'm not sleepy. I'm wide-awake." But then something in the look on Mommy and Daddy's faces and the tone of voice they used made Kim decide that she really had only one choice. "OK," she said. "Please give me a camel ride to bed."

So Daddy would carry her to bed and listen to her prayers. After Kim was snugly tucked in bed, Daddy would give her a big hug and kiss and whisper, "Good-night, wide-awake Kim."

Kim would lie for a long time, wide-awake, feeling the special corner of her blanket, listening to Mommy and Daddy talking and to the music playing and the telephone ringing and the dog barking and to all the night noises.

Sometimes, much later, Mommy would tiptoe back into Kim's room to make sure she was tucked in just right so she wouldn't roll out of the top bunk. She would lean over to give Kim a last good-night kiss, and exclaim, "Kim, are you still awake?" Kim just giggled and snuggled down farther under her soft blankets. And before long she dropped off to sleep.

When morning came, Kim was always the last one up. Sometimes she slept so long she almost missed breakfast.

Then one day little sister Kari was trying to wake Kim for breakfast. "Kim," she said, "you didn't get to go out with Daddy in the field today like I did. I saw a big rabbit and a gopher. And guess what—we found a big black dog that followed us all over."

"That's not fair," complained Kim as she sat down at the table. "Why didn't you take me?"

"You were sound asleep," said Daddy. "Kari goes to bed first, but she is also the first one up; so she can do special things with Mommy and me every morning."

"What does she get to do?" asked Kim.

"Well, the first thing she does is crawl into bed with Mommy and me while we are reading."

"Right," said Kari, "and I always get to hear a special story."

"That's not fair," said Kim. "I want a special story too. Tomorrow I'm getting up early, just like Kari."

"Early to bed—early to rise . . ." said Daddy.

When 8:00 bedtime came that night, Kevin was already asleep, Kari was already asleep, but Kim was wide-awake, as usual. So it was close to 9:00 before she finally crawled into bed. "Remember, Mommy, wake me up as soon as Kari gets up."

"OK," said Mommy. "Good-night."

It was a short night for Kim. Before she knew it, Mommy was shaking her. "Kim, get up. It's morning. Kari is already up, and Daddy is about to read her a special story in our bed."

Kim forced her eyes open, climbed down out of her top bunk, and crawled into bed beside Daddy. She almost fell asleep again halfway through the story, but she didn't want to miss anything this morning. Then after getting dressed, she and Kari helped Daddy feed the horses.

All day long Kim was sleepy, and finally she couldn't keep her eyes open any longer. Wide-awake

Kim was not wide-awake anymore. She was so sleepy she didn't even make it to bed. She fell sound asleep in her beanbag chair before Kevin or Kari even went to bed. Daddy carried her to her room and tucked her into bed for the night without Kim even knowing what was happening to her.

And who do you think was the first one up the next morning? That's right, wide-awake Kim.

She was the first one to crawl into bed with Daddy and Mommy; she was the first one to get a special morning story; she was the first one to go out exploring with Daddy in the field.

"It's fun to be the first one up," said Kim. "It's fun to be wide-awake in the morning. When 8:00 comes tonight, I'm going to jump right into bed so maybe I can be the first one up again tomorrow morning."

The Three Little Kittens

The three little kittens have lost their mommy and don't know what to do. Please, Mother dear, can't we have them?" Kim, Kari, and Kevin chanted as they danced around Mommy while she was trying to vacuum the floor.

Finally, Mommy turned off the sweeper and asked, "What kittens?"

"The wild kittens," they said.

"The wild kittens?"

"Yes, the three little wild kittens in the shed," said Kim.

And then Mommy remembered that Daddy had said that the wild mother cat that lived in the shed had had another litter of kittens.

"Oh, no," said Mommy. "Those kittens need their own mother."

"But the mommy cat hasn't been to the shed all day," said Kim.

"The babies need us or they might die," added Kari.

"Please, come see them, Mommy," begged the children as they grabbed Mommy's hands and led her to the shed.

"Mommy, see?" Kevin said, pointing to the three little bundles of fur in their bed of hay.

"Oh," said Mommy. "They are precious."

"That one's Calico," said Kim.

"That's Stripy," said Kari.

"And that's Boots," said Kevin.

"Please, please, can't we have them?" the children pleaded again.

"We'll see," said Mommy. "They look like they might be old enough to leave their mother. Let's take them into the house and see if they can drink milk from a dish."

"Goody! Goody!" the children exclaimed as they each picked up their favorite kitten.

Mommy poured some warm milk into a dish and put it down on the floor. The kittens looked at it— and walked away.

"Are they too small to drink milk from a dish?" asked Kim, with a worried look on her face.

"We'll see," said Mommy. "I don't think they know that milk comes in a dish. Put some milk on your finger and touch their noses," Mommy instructed.

The kittens licked the drop of milk off their noses—and walked away.

"How can we teach them to drink?"

"Dunk their noses in the milk," said Mommy.

"Really? Should we do that?" asked Kari.

"Try it," said Mommy.

So each child dunked a kitten's nose into the dish of milk.

Calico sneezed.

Stripy closed his eyes and jumped back so quickly that he rolled over.

Boots shook his head and whiskers, spraying milk all over the floor.

Then they each licked the milk from their noses, walked right up to the dish, and began drinking.

"Hurrah," Kim, Kari, and Kevin shouted. "They can drink milk from a dish."

"Please, Mother dear, can't we have them?"

"Well," said Mommy after a long thought, "I guess so."

The children smiled and clapped and again started dancing around Mommy, chanting,

"The three little kittens have lost their mommy,

And don't know what to do.

But, please, don't worry, little kittens,

We'll take care of you."

Then as Mommy went back to her vacuuming, Kim, Kari, and Kevin called, "Thank you, Mother dear!"

Kari Didn't Give Up

Oh, Mommy, do I have to go to swimming lessons again today?" complained Kari. "I hate swimming lessons. The water hurts my eyes. I get too tired. I wish you had never paid for the lessons, 'cause I don't want to go."

"I understand how you feel about swimming lessons," said Mommy. "But you do love to swim. And since I have already paid for the lessons, you need to go. Kim is waiting in the car."

Kari got into the car, but she wasn't very happy about it.

Kari went swimming, but she wasn't very happy about it.

Then the day came for the swimming test. Everyone who passed the test would get a special badge for his or her swimming suit and would get to go to the next class.

Kari wanted a badge.

Kari wanted to pass the test so she could go to the next class.

But the test was very hard. Kari tried, but she didn't pass. And what made it even worse was that her very own sister, Kim, did pass.

Kari was very sad that evening, and no one in the family mentioned swimming lessons because it made Kari cry.

After a few days Mommy asked Kari, "Do you want me to sign you up for swimming lessons again?" Mommy was quite sure Kari would say "NO!"

But to her surprise, Kari said, "Yes, I want to take swimming lessons so I can pass that test and be in the same class as Kim."

So Kari continued taking swimming lessons. She did just what the teacher told her to do.

She swam the length of the pool over and over again.

She practiced diving.

And as the weeks went by, Kari noticed something. She was swimming better. It was easier to swim the length of the pool. She didn't get tired. She could dive without doing a belly flop.

At last test day came again. This time Kari was ready.

The teacher said, "Swim for three minutes without touching the side of the pool." And Kari did it!

The teacher said, "Swim the length of the pool." And Kari did it!

The teacher said, "Dive into the water." And Kari did it!

Everything the teacher told Kari to do, she did!

Kari passed the test!

Kari got a badge for her swimming suit!

And Kari got to move up to the next class!

That afternoon the family celebrated Kari's success. They shouted, "Hip! Hip! Hurrah for Kari!"

And Kari was very glad she didn't give up.

The Empty Birthday Present

Soon it would be Daddy's birthday.

"Let's get Daddy a present," said Kim.

"A real neat present," said Kari.

"A big present," said Kevin.

What should they give Daddy?

"A bicycle," said Kim. "He could take us for rides." But a bicycle cost too much money.

"A big truck," said Kevin. "Daddy can play with me in the sandbox." But Daddy was too old to play in the sandbox.

"Candy," said Kari. "That special candy that Daddy likes."

"Oh, that hard candy with chocolate on it and nuts sprinkled on top; that comes in gold paper," said Kim.

"Yummy," said Kevin. "I love candy. I could eat it all up!"

Kim, Kari, and Kevin started saving their pennies, nickles, and dimes so they could buy Daddy some special candy for his birthday.

When shopping day came, they were ready with their money. At last Kim, Kari, and Kevin stood in front of the candy counter. They had never seen so much yummy-looking candy in their lives.

They knew candy could make holes in their teeth.

They knew too much candy would make them sick.

They knew Daddy didn't eat candy very often. But they knew he did like one special kind.

"There it is," said Kim. She reached high on the shelf and took down one box. They took it to the cashier and dumped their pennies, nickles, and dimes out on the counter.

"1, 2, 3, 4, 5 . . . 26, 27, 28 . . ." they counted. The cashier helped them. At last she said, "You have $1.22. You need one more dollar." Mommy opened her purse and gave the cashier a dollar. Kim, Kari, and Kevin carried the box of candy all the way home. "Daddy will love our present," they said.

When they got home, Mommy put the candy on the top shelf of the pantry. "It will be safe here," she said. "We'll wrap it later." And then Mommy went outside to water her garden.

"I bet that candy tastes yummy," said Kim.

"I bet it's the most delicious candy in the world," said Kari.

"I want some candy," said Kevin.

"It's Daddy's candy," said Kim. "But he probably wouldn't care if we took one piece."

"Let's get one," said Kari. "I'm hungry for candy. Nobody will ever know."

So Kim got the tall stool and pushed it into the pantry. She climbed up and reached just as high as she could. She took the box of candy, opened it, and took out one piece.

"I want one piece just for me," said Kari. So Kim took out one more piece.

"I want one too," said Kevin. So Kim took out one more piece.

Then she put the top back on the box and put the box back on the top shelf of the pantry, just as it was before.

And Kim, Kari, and Kevin each ate one piece of Daddy's birthday candy.

The next day when Kim, Kari, and Kevin walked past the pantry, they thought about Daddy's birthday candy. It tasted so good. Mommy was busy writing a letter in the study. She would never know. So up climbed Kim. She took three more

pieces out of the box, put the top back on the box,
and climbed down again.

    And she did the same thing the next day,
        and the next day,
            and the next day,
                until the box was empty.

Then it was Daddy's birthday. It was time to wrap Daddy's birthday present. Mommy reached up high, high on the very top shelf of the pantry. There was the candy box, right where she had put it. She took it down. She wrapped it in pretty red paper and put a big white bow on it.

When the children saw the pretty package, they asked, "What's in it?"

"That's the special box of candy that you children bought for Daddy's birthday," said Mommy.

"But we can't give Daddy that present," said Kim.

"Why not?" asked Mommy.

"Because it's empty," said Kari.

"It's empty!" exclaimed Mommy.

"We ate it all up," said Kevin.

"We'll have to buy Daddy another present," said Kim.

"I'm sorry," said Mommy. "It's too late."

"What can we do?" cried the children. "We want to give Daddy a present."

"You can give Daddy this pretty wrapped present," said Mommy.

"But it's empty!"

"Then you will just have to tell Daddy why you are giving him an empty present," said Mommy.

When Daddy came home from work that night, Kim, Kari, and Kevin sang "Happy Birthday to Daddy," and then they gave him the pretty wrapped present.

Daddy took off the paper, opened the box, and looked inside.

"What is it?" he asked.

"It's an empty present," said Kim.

"We ate it," said Kevin.

"Without asking," said Kari.

"We're very sorry," they said. "We'll never give you an empty birthday present again."

And they never did!

The Day
Oma Came Home

Oma was Kim, Kari, and Kevin's grandmother.

Oma had been very sick. She had to spend many weeks in the hospital. But today she was coming home. She wasn't going to her own house. She was coming to Kim, Kari, and Kevin's house to live until she was stronger.

"Where do you think Oma should sleep?" Mommy asked the children.

"Your bed is the biggest," said Kim. "Maybe she could sleep with you and Daddy."

"I don't think that would work," said Mommy. "Oma needs a bed of her own."

"She can sleep in my bed," said Kim, "and I could sleep with Kari."

"But you and Kari always fight over the covers and kick each other out of bed when you try to sleep together. And besides, I don't think Oma could climb up the ladder to your top bunk bed."

"She can sleep in my room," said Kevin.

"That's the best idea I've heard so far," said Mommy. "We could move Kevin's crib and clothes and toys into Kim and Kari's bedroom and move the extra bed that is stored in the garage into Kevin's room for Oma."

"That's a good idea," echoed the children. "When will Oma be here?"

"Soon," said Mommy, starting to push Kevin's crib through the door.

"May I help you?" asked Kim.

"Yes," said Mommy. "Help me guide the other end of this crib through the door."

"What can I do?" asked Kari.

"You may start bringing in Kevin's clothes and hanging them in one side of your closet."

"Me too," said Kevin.

"OK, Kevin. You can move your toys from the toy shelf in your room to the toy shelf in Kim and Kari's room."

The children carried load after load from Kevin's room into Kim and Kari's room. Finally Kevin's room was empty, and the other room was full.

"When will Oma be here?"

"Soon," said Mommy, moving the extra bed from the garage into Oma's new room.

"What else can we do?" asked the children.

"Kim, you can get a pitcher of cold water and a clean glass."

"Kari, you can cut some flowers and put them in a vase."

"Kevin, you can help me make this bed for Oma."

Just as the children finished their jobs, they heard a car in the driveway.

"Oma's here," they shouted as they rushed out to greet her.

"Hi, Oma, you get to sleep in Kevin's room," they called.

"I put a pitcher of water by your bed," said Kim.

"And I picked some beautiful flowers for your room," said Kari.

"I made your bed," said Kevin.

Daddy helped Oma into the wheelchair, and the girls pushed her wheelchair toward the house, while Kevin got a free ride.

"What a pretty room!" Oma exclaimed. "Is this room just for me?"

"Yes," said Kim. "Kevin gets to sleep in our room."

"I'm a big boy now," said Kevin.

"It's going to be fun sleeping in one room," said Kari.

Soon bedtime came. Oma was very tired.

Kim gave her a drink of water.

Kari put her glasses on the table by the flowers.

And Kevin pulled down the covers on her bed— and crawled in.

"I'm just warming up Oma's bed," said Kevin.

After Oma was tucked into bed beside Kevin, Kari crawled in. "I just want to give Oma a back rub," said Kari.

And then Kim crawled in. "I just want to tell Oma a bedtime story," said Kim.

And by the time Mommy finished washing the supper dishes and Daddy finished feeding the dogs, what do you think they found when they looked into Oma's room?

There was Kevin,
        and Kari,
            and Kim,
                and Oma, all sound asleep in one bed.

No More Diddle-daddling

Girls, you must clean your room today."

"Oh, Mommy. Do we have to?" said Kari.

"It's too messy. We can't clean up all this junk," said Kim.

"Who got it all out?" asked Mommy.

"We did. But it will take us a week to get it put back."

"Well, then, you had better get started," said Mommy.

Kim and Kari went into their room. "Ugh!" they groaned. "What a mess!"

There was a pile of dirty clothes right where Kim and Kari had stepped out of their clothes the night before.

There were at least 10 dolls on top of things, under things, and in things.

Socks were scattered on the floor, where Kari had dumped them out. She had been trying to find two alike.

Three puzzles had been started but never finished.

And then there were pencils and paper and pens and—

"This is impossible," said Kim, sitting down on the beanbag chair next to her favorite doll. "My dolly needs some clothes on first." She went over to the doll-clothes drawer and selected a dress, hat, sweater, and booties for her doll.

Kari sat down on the floor and spied the paper basket she had started to make. "It still needs a handle," she said. "I guess I'll do that first."

About an hour later, Mommy called, "How's your room coming, girls?"

"Fine," they said.

Kim put the doll in the baby buggy, and Kari put her finished basket on the shelf. But they still hadn't touched the dirty clothes, the other nine dolls, the socks, the three half-finished puzzles, and the pencils and paper and pens.

"I'm tired of cleaning," said Kim.

"Me too," said Kari. "Let's make a bed in the top of the closet."

"That's a good idea," said Kim.

So they propped the bunk-bed ladder against the wall and climbed up to the top of the closet.

"We can put our dollies to sleep up here," said Kim, smoothing out a blanket.

Up and down the ladder they went, carrying up blankets and pillows and six dolls.

About a half hour later, Mommy called, "How's your room coming, girls?"

"Fine," they said.

But they still hadn't touched the dirty clothes, the other three dolls, the socks, the three half-finished puzzles, and the pencils and paper and pens.

Just then the telephone rang, and the girls could hear Mommy saying, "Oh, how exciting! Yes, I think the children would love to go. Two o'clock? I think we can make it. The girls must finish cleaning their room before we can go. But they have been working on it for over an hour and a half now. It should be almost finished. See you soon. Goodbye."

"Who was that?" the girls called from their perch in the top of the closet.

"That was Aunt Joanie. She and Uncle Dick are going to the mountains for a picnic, and she thought you children might like to go along."

"Yippee, yippee, yippee," the girls shouted. "When can we go?"

"We need to leave in an hour. But your room must be spic and span before that time, or you won't be able to go."

"Oh, what will we do?" cried Kari, looking down on the mess below.

"No more diddle-daddling around," said Kim. "Let's get this place clean. Mommy means what she says."

And in less than six minutes Kim and Kari had

carried down all the blankets and pillows and dolls from the top of the closet.

And in two more minutes the dirty clothes had been picked up and put in the dirty-clothes basket in the bathroom.

It took only seven minutes to find all of the ten dolls and line them up neatly on the shelf.

Putting all the loose socks together was a job. But in 10 minutes they were all put away in the sock drawer.

Now the puzzles. Kim and Kari each chose one to put together. It took them nine minutes. They decided to cooperate on the last puzzle, and it took only six minutes to finish putting that one together.

Now all that was left were the pencils and paper and pens. They put the pencils in the pencil box, and the pens in the pen box, and the drawings in one pile, and the clean paper in another pile, and the mussed-up paper in the wastebasket. That job was finished in 10 minutes.

Then they jumped up and looked around the room and shouted, "We're finished!"

"Good," said Mommy. "You have 10 minutes left to change your clothes, comb your hair, get your sweaters, and get into the car."

In less than 10 minutes they were on their way to the mountains.

"I thought you girls said it would take a week to clean your room," said Mommy.

Kim and Kari started to giggle as they answered, "That depends on whether you diddle-daddle or not."

Where's Kevin?

Kevin was a baby.

Kevin was a boy.

Everyone loved Kevin.

When Kevin was tiny, Mommy and Daddy would carry him everywhere they went.

Upstairs.

Downstairs.

Inside.

Outside.

When Mommy and Daddy stopped to talk, Kim and Kari would say, "Let us hold Kevin."

And all the people would stop talking and look at Kevin's sisters and say, "My, what big girls you are, to be able to carry your brother!"

Kevin kept growing.
One day he rolled over.
One day he crawled.
And one day he walked.
Kevin was still a baby.
Kevin was still a boy.
And everyone still loved
Kevin, but they no longer car-
ried him wherever they went.

One day after church, Mommy and Daddy stopped to talk with old friends.

They talked,
   and they talked,
      and they talked.

When they finished talking, it was very late and guests were waiting to ride home with the family for dinner.

"Come, children!" Daddy called. He took Kim and Kari by the hand and started walking toward the car. Mommy said, as mommies sometimes do, she wanted to say one more thing and then she would meet everyone at the car.

Mommy finished saying her one more thing and

ran to the car, just as everyone was getting into the car. Mommy found a place in the back seat, and Kim and Kari crawled on her lap. Away they went toward home.

About a mile down the road, Daddy asked, "You have Kevin on your lap, don't you?"

"No," said Mommy, "Kevin is up in the front seat with you, isn't he?"

"No," said Daddy, "I thought he was with you."

"No," said Mommy, "I thought he was with you."

"Where's Kevin?" everyone asked.

"He must still be at church."

And before you could blink an eye, Daddy screeched the brakes and turned the car around in the middle of the street and raced back to the church.

There was Kevin, sitting on the church steps
with two little children,
talking,
and talking,
and talking—baby talk.

"Hi," said Kevin as he saw all his family come
running up to him.

Mommy picked him up first and hugged and
kissed him and cried for joy, because she had found
her lost baby boy.

Daddy picked him up
and carried him all the
way to the car.

Then Kim and Kari picked him up and held him as they rode home.

Kevin was still a baby.

Kevin was still a boy.

Everyone still loved Kevin—but the next time Mommy and Daddy stopped to talk, you can be sure everyone kept an eye on Kevin, and everyone remembered to take him home.

Kim's Ride Home

Kim, Kari, and Kevin were playing with their friends in the park.

"Time to go home. Come quickly," called Mommy.

"I don't want to go home," said Kevin from the top of the jungle gym.

"I don't want to go home," said Kari from the swinging swing.

"I don't want to go home," said Kim from her bicycle.

"I know you have had a good time at the park, but we must go home right now. Aunt Joanie and cousin Timmy may be there any time. I don't want to miss them."

"OK," said Kevin as he climbed down from the jungle gym.

"OK," said Kari as she stopped her swing.

"No," said Kim, "I want to get a drink at the restroom."

"You can get one at home. It will take us only a few minutes to get there."

"No," said Kim, "I want to get one now."

"Come now or I will have to leave you, and you will have to come home with your friends," warned Mommy.

"No," said Kim as she pedaled her bike around the corner of the restroom building and disappeared.

What should Mommy do?

Kevin and Kari were in the car just as they were supposed to be. But Kim was in the restroom, just where she wasn't supposed to be.

After Mommy told the friends in the park what she was planning to do, Mommy got into the car, started the motor, and drove home, leaving Kim behind. Mommy had decided to leave a note for Aunt Joanie on the front door of their house to tell her where they were and then come back for Kim.

Kim took her time getting a nice long drink at the water fountain, and then she decided she needed to wash her hands. She turned on the water and squirted soap on her hands. Then she washed and washed until the soap bubbles spilled down into the sink. Then she rinsed every bubble away. She reached for a paper towel and wiped and wiped and wiped until every drop of water had disappeared.

Then she got another long drink at the water fountain. Finally she got on her bike and peddled to the parking lot where she was sure Mommy was waiting.

But Mommy was not there!

Kari was not there!

Kevin was not there!

The car was gone!

Kim looked around. Her friends were still playing on the jungle gym. But she wanted to see Aunt Joanie and cousin Timmy. She wanted to go home. She was hungry. She was tired. Tears started trickling down her cheeks. What should she do?

Kim knew where home was. It was just a few blocks away. But it was a long way for a little girl to go on a bicycle all by herself.

She started pedaling.

She reached the first corner.

She looked both ways.

She walked her bike across the street.

She wiped a tear from her cheek.

She got on her bike again.

She started pedaling.

Then a car pulled to the side of the road, and someone called to her, "Little girl, do you need a ride home?"

She kept pedaling, not even looking around.

The man called louder, "Little girl, do you need a ride?"

Kim kept pedaling.

Finally the man said, "Kim, do you want me to take you home?"

This time Kim looked around. There was Daddy.

"Daddy, oh, Daddy! Is that really you?" Kim said, as she stopped her bike, ran to his waiting arms, and blew her nose in his handkerchief.

Daddy put her bicycle in the back of the car, and Kim told him the whole story as they drove home. Mommy was just leaving for the park when they turned into the driveway, and Kim ended her story by saying, "and I'll never disobey Mommy again."

Don't Call Me "Baby"!

It's Thursday," said Mommy. "Time for story hour at the library."

Oh, how Kim and Kari loved story hour. The librarian always gave them special name tags and read them special stories—and no mommies and daddies were allowed. Kim and Kari got to go all by themselves. They felt very grown-up.

Mommy waved goodbye from the car as Kim and Kari skipped up the walk to the library. "See you in an hour," she called. "Have a good time."

"Goodbye," they called as they pulled open the big library door and walked in.

The library was a very special place. Kim and Kari sat down at a table to wait for story hour to begin.

Soon the librarian came with some books in one hand and name tags in the other. She called each child's name. Finally she called, "Kari Kuzma."

"Here I am," said Kari, jumping to her feet.

The librarian carefully placed a name tag with her name printed on it in big letters around Kari's neck.

Then the librarian called, "Kim Kuzma."

"That's me," said Kim.

The librarian carefully placed the name tag with Kim Kuzma printed on it in big letters around Kim's neck.

Now everyone who could read would know that Kari was Kari Kuzma. Nobody else had that special

name. And everyone who could read would know that Kim was Kim Kuzma. Nobody else had that special name.

"It's time to go into the special story-hour room," said the librarian. "Follow me."

Kim and Kari held hands as they followed the other children into the special room. They found a place on the rug and sat down to listen. A big girl sat down beside them. Kari looked up and smiled and the girl said, "Hi, little baby."

"Don't call me a baby," said Kari.

"But you are one. You're just a baby," said the big girl.

Kari didn't like being called a baby, so she whispered to Kim, "Let's move."

Kim and Kari got up and walked to the other side of the room and again sat down on the rug.

The librarian began reading. She read a story about a boy who had a bear for a pet. She read a story about a farmer who lost his hat. She read a story about a duck family trying to find a place to build a nest. Then it was time for the children to check out books that they wanted to take home. Kim and Kari held hands and walked back to the children's section of the library. The big girl followed them.

"Hi, babies," the girl called.

"Don't pay any attention," Kim whispered to Kari as they walked on.

"You're both babies. Babies, babies, babies," she chanted after them.

"We are not!" said Kari, starting to cry.

"See, ha, ha. Crybaby is your name."

"No, it isn't," said Kim. "This name tag says my name is Kim Kuzma. My sister's name is Kari Kuzma. And we are not babies!"

Just then Mommy opened the library door, and Kim and Kari ran to her.

"What's the matter?" Mommy asked, seeing tears in Kari's eyes.

"That big girl was teasing us," said Kim.

"She called us babies," said Kari.

And then Mommy said, "You are what you believe you are. No matter what anyone calls you. Remember, you belong to Daddy and me. We love you. Your family name is Kuzma. You can be proud of that. You are special. And no one calling you names will ever change that."

Baby-sitting Timmy

Mommy and Daddy were going on a trip. They were going to be gone for five days. They had work to do. They had to attend meetings. So Kim, Kari, and Kevin were going to stay with their cousins.

"I'm going to play with Timmy," said Kevin as he put his blocks and books and cars and trucks and blanket into a suitcase.

"I'm going to play with Chares," said Kim as she packed her dolls and doll clothes and crayons and coloring books and puzzles into a suitcase.

"Kari, where would you like to stay?" asked Mommy. "You have your choice. You may stay at Chares's house, or you may stay at Timmy's house."

Kari thought and thought. It would be a lot of fun to play with Chares. But Chares was Kim's age, and she had two older brothers. Kari would be the littlest in the family if she went there.

Timmy was a baby—even smaller than Kevin. She would be the biggest one in the family if she went there.

Kari thought and thought. And then she said, "I'm going to stay with Timmy. I'll be the baby-sitter. Aunt Joanie isn't used to having two little boys. She can baby-sit Kevin, and I'll baby-sit Timmy."

The more Kari thought about the idea, the more excited she became. "I'm going to baby-sit Timmy," she sang as she packed some books just for Timmy and a ball just for Timmy and a doll just for Timmy.

Soon it was time for Mommy and Daddy to leave. The children packed the car with the suitcases and toys that they wanted to take to their cousins.

The first stop was at Chares's house. "Have a good time. We love you," called Mommy and Daddy as they waved goodbye to Kim.

The next stop was at Timmy's house. "Have a good time. We love you," called Mommy and Daddy as they waved goodbye to Kevin and Kari.

Kari ran up to Timmy and gave him a great big hug. "I'm going to be your baby-sitter for five whole

days. Look what I brought for you," Kari said as she opened her suitcase full of toys for Timmy.

"Book," said Timmy.

"Do you want me to read you a story?" Kari asked eagerly.

"Ball," said Timmy.

"Do you want me to play ball with you?" Kari asked eagerly.

"Baby," said Timmy.

"Do you want me to play baby doll with you?" Kari asked eagerly.

"Dinnertime," called Aunt Joanie.

"I'll wash Timmy's hands and face," Kari said. Aunt Joanie washed Kevin's.

"Naptime," called Aunt Joanie.

"I'll put Timmy to bed," Kari said. Aunt Joanie put Kevin to bed.

"Parktime," called Aunt Joanie.

"I'll push Timmy's stroller," Kari said. Aunt Joanie held Kevin's hand.

Kari was so interested in her baby-sitting job that before she knew it,

Monday passed,

and Tuesday passed,

and Wednesday passed,

and Thursday passed,

and it was Friday.

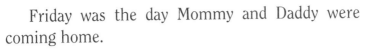

Friday was the day Mommy and Daddy were coming home.

Beep, beep!

"Here they are!" shouted Kari as she rushed out to the car.

After hugs and kisses Mommy and Daddy asked, "Did you have a good time?"

"A wonderful time," said Kari, "and the very best was baby-sitting Timmy."

There They Blow!

There they blow! There they blow!" Kim yelled as she pointed across the water. "What are they?"

"Porpoises," said Daddy.

"Sea lions," said Mommy.

"Killer whales," said Kari.

"Monsters," said Kevin.

"Whatever they are, I wish they would swim over here. I wouldn't be afraid," said Kim bravely.

"Me either!" said Kevin boldly.

"I would," said Kari timidly. "I'd rather go shelling with Grandma and Grandpa."

The next day Mommy and Daddy decided to paddle the little rubber canoe across the bay to a small island. "Anybody want to go along?" Daddy asked.

"I do," said Kim.

"I do," said Kevin.

"I don't," said Kari. "I'd rather go shelling with Grandma and Grandpa!"

So Kim and Kevin climbed into the canoe, while Kari picked up her bucket and started walking down the beach looking for pretty shells. Daddy paddled away from shore, and as they looked back, Kari and Grandma and Grandpa grew smaller and smaller. Soon the canoe was so far away that they couldn't even be seen.

Beyond the sheltered cove the wind blew the

water into white-capped waves that rocked the canoe back and forth. Kevin snuggled deep into the canoe to find shelter from the wind and promptly fell asleep.

Then suddenly Kim saw the black sea creatures coming straight toward the canoe. "There they blow! There they blow!" Kim screamed. She forgot all about her brave statement just the day before. "What if they are porpoises—? Or sea lions—? Or killer whales—? Or monsters? Let's go back. Quick! Quick! Let's get out of here."

"We can't," said Mommy and Daddy. "There is no place to go. But don't worry. They are just porpoises," Daddy said as the black sea creatures came closer.

"Just porpoises!" Kim screamed above the wind. "I'm scared!"

She remembered the stories told about the curious porpoises that sometimes come right up to boats and nuzzle them. "They are coming closer! They are going to tip over the boat! Help! Help!" Kim shouted. "We're surrounded!"

"Just pray," said Mommy, trying to keep calm. "We

can't do anything ourselves now. We're surrounded."

Kim whispered a prayer. Daddy stopped paddling as the school of porpoises swam around the canoe. Kim dug her fingernails into the side of the canoe as she sat, frozen with fear, watching them dive and blow on all sides.

Finally, just as gracefully as they had dived toward the canoe, they dived past it and headed on to their feeding grounds. Kevin was still asleep as Kim called after the retreating porpoises, "There they blow! There they blow!"

The call woke Kevin. "What is it? What is it?" he asked sleepily.

"Porpoises," said Kim.

"Where are they?"

"They're gone," said Kim. "But just a minute ago a whole school of them were all around us!"

"Really?" said Kevin, wide-awake now.

But it was too late, the porpoises were gone.

After exploring the island, Daddy paddled the tiny canoe back through the wind and the waves to shore, where Kari and Grandma and Grandpa were waiting with Kim's bucket full of shells.

"You should have come with us," said Kim. "A whole school of porpoises swam around our canoe!"

"Is that true?" Kari inquired.

"Yes, and I was scared," said Kim humbly.

"I wasn't scared," said Kevin boldly. (He forgot to mention that he was sleeping.)

Kari stopped and thought. "I probably would have been scared too," she said. And then she added, "I'd rather go shelling with Grandma and Grandpa. And besides, we found three big sand dollars!"

Making Friends
With Andy

Kari liked her teacher.
Kari liked the toys.
Kari liked the stories.
Kari liked her classmates.
Kari liked playing inside.

But there was one thing Kari did not like at nursery school. Kari did not like to play outside.

Kari did not like to play outside because Andy was always outside.

Andy was a big boy from another class. Andy liked to fight.

He liked to fight big boys and
big girls.

He liked to fight little boys and
little girls.

He even liked to fight Kari. But Kari did not like
to fight.

Kari liked just to play peacefully,
making sand pies in the sandbox,
or being an acrobat on the jungle gym,
or jumping rope.

But as soon as Andy would see Kari making sand

109

pies in the sandbox, he would run over and smash them.

And as soon as Andy would see Kari playing acrobat on the jungle gym, he would run over and pull her hair.

And as soon as Andy would see Kari jumping rope, he would grab the rope away from her and run.

One day Kari's friend Mark brought some gum to school for his birthday. There were enough pieces for each child in the class.

There was one for Bryan,
one for Jennifer,
one for Troy,
one for Vonnie,
one for Jeffrey,
one for Rodney,
one for Tracy,
one for Brittany,
one for Timothy,
one for Melonee,
one for Rachelle,
and one for Kari.

Andy walked by, and when he saw everyone chewing gum he said, "I want some gum."

But the gum was all gone.

The next day on the way to nursery school, Kari asked, "Daddy, may I have a piece of gum?"

"You already have one piece of gum," said Daddy.

"I know, but I need one more," said Kari.

"What for?" asked Daddy.

"For Andy," said Kari.

"Who's Andy?" asked Daddy.

"I'll show you," said Kari.

When Daddy and Kari got to nursery school, they walked right past Kari's classroom. They walked right past the next classroom, until they came to Andy's classroom.

Daddy knocked on the door.

Andy's teacher opened the door. "May I help you?" she asked.

"We would like to see Andy," Daddy said.

Andy was very surprised when he came to the door and saw Kari and her daddy.

"Daddy, this is Andy."

"Hi," said Daddy. "It's nice to meet you."

"Hi," said Andy.

"Here is some gum," said Kari.

"For me?" asked Andy. He was very surprised.

"Yes," said Kari.

"Thanks," said Andy.

Kari went to her room.

She played with toys.

She listened to stories.

She played with her classmates.

But all the time she played inside she kept won-

dering what would happen when she went outside. Would Andy still try to fight with her?

When it was outside time, Kari went to the sandbox to make sand pies. Andy came over. "Can I have a taste?" asked Andy. They both giggled.

Kari played acrobat on the jungle gym. Andy came over. "Are you going to be in a circus?" asked Andy. They both giggled.

Kari started jumping rope. Andy came over. "Can I jump with you?" asked Andy. Andy took one jump, tripped, and fell over. They both giggled.

Kari still liked her teacher,
   the toys,
      the stories,
         her classmates,
            and playing inside.

But now Kari liked something else. Kari liked playing outside because Andy was there. And Andy was her friend.

Sarnoff

Sarnoff was a prayed-for puppy. Daddy had promised Kim, Kari, and Kevin that they could have a Doberman puppy out of Liza's next litter, if there was a handsome boy pup.

The children began praying, "Dear Jesus, help Liza to have a good little boy puppy so we can have it for our very own. Amen."

Finally the day came. Seven puppies were born.

"Daddy, are there any handsome little boy puppies?"

"I can't believe it," said Daddy. "Liza had six boy puppies and only one little girl puppy. I think there just might be one here for you."

The puppies grew. Their eyes opened. They started walking on their wobbly legs. They started eating puppy food from a dish. And all this time there was one puppy that stood out from the others. He had a beautiful head, a big chest, and strong legs, and he was smart. Everyone who came to look at the puppies said that he was sure to become a champion.

"Can we have that special puppy?" the children begged.

"Yes," said Daddy. "We'll call him Sarnoff."

Oh, how the children loved their puppy, Sarnoff.

Finally, one by one, all the puppies but three were selected by daddies and mommies and little boys and girls to go to new homes. Sarnoff, Comet, and Classy were the only puppies left. Whenever the family would come home, Liza and her three puppies would bark at the fence and jump around welcoming them. The children loved all the puppies, but they loved Sarnoff best of all, because they knew they could keep him for their very own.

One day when the family came home, there were only two puppies barking beside Liza. Sarnoff was missing. "Where's Sarnoff?" everyone cried.

"Sarnoff! Sarnoff! Come, Sarnoff!" the children called as they walked around the yard. It was dark out and very hard to see a little black puppy who might be hiding in the yard. But no puppy came bounding out of the shadows. Daddy and Mommy walked the fence to see if Sarnoff had dug a hole under the fence and run away. But there wasn't any hole.

Finally, Daddy said, "I think I had better get my great big flashlight and go look for Sarnoff in the orange groves. He must be there someplace. You children go in with Mommy and start getting into bed."

Nobody wanted to go to bed that night. But it was late, and Mommy said they must. As the children knelt down to pray, Kim had an idea. "I know what we'll do; we'll ask Jesus to help Daddy find Sarnoff."

So Kim prayed, "Dear Jesus, please help Daddy find Sarnoff."

And Kari prayed, "Dear Jesus, please help Sarnoff to come back home."

And Kevin prayed, "Jesus, Amen," because he was just a baby.

Late that night after the children were all asleep, Daddy came home without Sarnoff.

The next day the children played with Comet and Classy, but it wasn't the same. They missed Sarnoff. When the next day passed and still Sarnoff hadn't come home, Mommy and Daddy gave up hope. They thought they would never see Sarnoff again. But the children kept praying.

The next day the children heard a friend tell Daddy that he should put a notice in the paper about losing the puppy and offer a reward and then someone might return him. Daddy seemed doubtful, but the children pleaded, "Please, please, Daddy, put it in the paper. Jesus will help us find Sarnoff."

So Daddy put an ad in the paper that said, "Lost Doberman puppy. Reward $100."

Every time the telephone rang, the children ran to see if someone was calling about Sarnoff.

Finally one day the telephone rang, and a man said, "I think I have found your dog."

"Tell us about the dog you found," Mommy said.

"Well, *she* is a very nice dog—"

"Oh, I'm sorry," said Mommy. "You did not find our dog, because our dog is a *he,* not a *she.*"

Again the telephone rang, and a boy said, "I think I have found your dog." But the dog he found was a big dog with short ears and a long tail, and Sarnoff was a little dog with long ears and a short tail.

Two weeks went by, and Daddy was just about to call the newspaper office and tell them to cancel the

ad, when one night Mommy answered the phone and a lady said, "I think I know where your lost dog is."

"Wonderful," said Mommy. "Tell me more about the dog."

So the lady continued, "Two weeks ago my neighbors brought home a nice-looking, male Doberman puppy. . . ."

"Oh," said Mommy, "that sounds just like our dog. What is your name so we can send you the reward, if indeed it is our dog?"

But the lady said, "I don't want a reward. I just want you to be happy and find the dog you are looking for."

Now Kim, Kari, and Kevin did not know about

this telephone call because they were getting ready for bed. And quietly, without telling the children, Daddy went to see if the dog was really Sarnoff.

Just as Mommy finished reading three bedtime stories (one for each child) and just as Kim, Kari, and Kevin were about to kneel down to say their prayers, who do you think came barking and bouncing through the house and jumped right up on the sofa—right where he wasn't supposed to be?

Yes, you guessed it. It was Sarnoff!

"Jesus answered our prayers. Our Sarnoff has come home! Daddy, Mommy, Sarnoff is home!" the children shouted.

"Yes," said Daddy. "How would you like to hear another bedtime story—this time the story about how Jesus answered *your* prayers." Then Daddy sat down and told the children about the telephone call and how he jumped into the car and drove to a house and went up to the door and knocked and when a lady opened the door, there was Sarnoff!

"Apparently," said Daddy, "three boys were walking by our house one day, and when they saw the puppies they wanted one. They thought it wouldn't hurt to take a puppy home for themselves since there would still be two left. So they took a rope and put it around Sarnoff's head as he jumped at the fence, and then they lifted him right out of the yard and took him home. They told their mother that a friend of theirs had given them the dog. They thought nobody had seen them and no one would ever know. But Jesus had seen them. And a neighbor had seen them."

"And I'm just sure," continued Daddy, "that when Jesus heard the prayers that you children prayed every night, He helped that neighbor lady to read the paper and see the notice about the lost dog and then to call us."

And right then they all knelt down again and

Kim prayed, "Dear Jesus, thank You for helping Daddy find Sarnoff."

And Kari prayed, "Dear Jesus, thank You for helping Sarnoff to come back home."

And Kevin prayed, "Jesus, Amen," because he was just a baby.

Jesus hears the prayers of all His children, even the baby ones.

The Ladder of Life Series

Help your children develop the Christian virtues mentioned by Peter in 2 Peter 1:5-7 (faith, virtue, temperance, patience, love, etc.) by using The Ladder of Life *Activity and Song Book,* storybooks, and cassettes.

As your children listen to the character-building stories, sing the delightful songs, and engage in the creative learning activities, they'll develop a friendship with Jesus and a desire to reflect His character.

Activity and Song Book
Contains learning activities that range in complexity for ages birth through early elementary, memory verses that reinforce the character traits, songs with easy-to-play piano accompaniment, and discussion questions. Paper, US$9.99, Cdn$14.49.

Storybooks
Eight storybooks for children based on the character traits in 2 Peter 1:5-7. Each story is about 5-6 pages long. The pictures can be colored. Paper, US$31.99, Cdn$46.49 set.

Activity and Song Book and eight storybooks, US$39.99, Cdn$57.99.

Cassettes
Features stories and songs. US$6.99, Cdn$9.99 each.
US$23.99, Cdn$34.99 set of four.

Available at all ABC Christian bookstores **(1-800-765-6955)** and other Christian bookstores. Prices and availability subject to change. Add GST in Canada.